The
BALLGAME
WITH NO ONE AT BAT

by
Steve Brezenoff

illustrated by
Marcos Calo

STONE ARCH BOOKS
a capstone imprint

r Samantha Archer,

Field Trip Mysteries are published by Stone Arch Books
A Capstone Imprint
1710 Roe Crest Drive
North Mankato, Minnesota 55603
www.capstonepub.com

Library of Congress Cataloging-in-Publication Data
Brezenoff, Steven.
   The ballgame with no one at bat / by Steve Brezenoff;
illustrated by Marcos Calo.
       p. cm. -- (Field trip mysteries)
   ISBN 978-1-4342-5978-3 (library binding)
   ISBN 978-1-4342-6211-0 (pbk.)
1. School field trips--Juvenile fiction. 2. Minor league
baseball--Juvenile fiction. 3. Theft--Juvenile fiction. [1.
Mystery and detective stories. 2. School field trips--Fiction.
3. Baseball--Fiction. 4. Theft--Fiction.] I. Calo, Marcos, ill.
II. Title. III. Series: Brezenoff, Steven. Field trip mysteries.
   PZ7.B7576Bal 2013                        2012049374
   813.6--dc23

Graphic Designer: Kristi Carlson

Summary: Edward "Egg" Garrison and his friends are on a field trip to watch the local minor league baseball team, but a theft at the concession stand is delaying the game, so the four sixth-grade detectives decide to investigate.

Printed in China.
032013    007228RRDF13

# TABLE OF CONTENTS

**Edward G. Garrison**

A.K.A: Egg

D.O.B: May 14th

POSITION: 6th Grade

*This can't be correct.
Please confirm.*

**INTERESTS:**
Photography, field trips

**KNOWN ASSOCIATES:**
Archer, Samantha; Duran, Catalina;
and Shoo, James.

**NOTES:**
Ms. Stanwyck encourages Edward's
passion for photography, but some
teachers complain of the frequent
use of the flash.

*Is photography allowed in school? I will
look into this.*

## OUT TO THE BALLGAME

"The colors are very pretty,
aren't they?" said Cat Duran.
I nodded. The trees exploded in
yellow, orange, and red.
"I got a lot of great photos of the
trees along the river
this weekend," I said.

"I'd like to see those pictures, Egg," Cat said, smiling. Everyone calls me Egg because my initials are E. G. G., for Edward G. Garrison.

I pulled off my camera to show her the images on the screen. "They'll look better when I print them," I said.

"Ooh, can I see too?" said a snotty voice next to me. It was Anton Gutman, my least favorite sixth grader.

He stood there, laughing at us. "You dorks," he said. "I bet you don't know anything about baseball. Why are you even on this trip?"

He meant our field trip to see the River City River Rats play. They're our minor-league baseball team. The sixth-grade gym class goes to a game every year.

Anton was right. I didn't know much about baseball, or any sport for that matter. But I was still excited to go. Baseball makes for great photos.

"Go away, Anton," said Sam Archer, standing up. She sat in the seat across the aisle with Gum Shoo. They were Cat's and my other best friends.

Sam's the tallest kid in sixth grade. So when she stood up and put her hands on her hips, she was pretty intimidating to Anton.

Anton gulped, but then he pretended he wasn't worried. He grinned up at her. "Okay, dork protector," he said. "I'll leave the four dorks alone so they can cry."

Then, with a loud snort, he headed toward the front of the bus and sat down with his dad. His father was helping chaperone the trip.

"Don't listen to him," said Peter Laurie from the seat in front of us. "That guy's a jerk."

"Oh, we know," I said. "He's our arch enemy."

"Mine too," said Peter. "When he heard that my dad got laid off, he made up a whole big rhyme about how poor we were. I got mad at first, but now I just ignore it."

"That's a good plan," said Cat.

"Yeah," said Peter. "And it works. He hasn't bugged me in days." He smiled, then turned around and dropped back into his seat.

Sitting behind us was the other chaperone: Cat's dad. He'd fallen asleep right when the bus pulled away from the school. Now he was slumped over, snoring.

"He's so embarrassing," Cat said to me.

"I don't know," I said. "My dad snores too."

"But not in front of the whole class!" Cat pointed out.

The bus jerked to a stop in front of the stadium. Our gym teacher, Mr. Jump, stood up in the front seat and faced the class. "Here we are," he said. "Everyone get off, quickly and quietly."

His voice woke up Mr. Duran. He coughed and sat upright. "Oh, are we here already?" he said. "What a quick trip!"

"Sure, Dad," said Cat. "Of course it's quick when you're asleep the whole time."

"Huh?" said her dad. "I wasn't sleeping. I was just resting my eyes."

"Yeah, and exercising your nose!" said Gum quietly to me and Sam.

We climbed down from the bus and got a look at the stadium. It wasn't a big stadium. It only held around six thousand people — way fewer than the big stadiums they use for the majors.

"This is gonna be great," said Sam. "The cool, autumn afternoon. Bright sunshine. And the best game mankind ever invented!"

Sam's a bit of a baseball fan, in case it wasn't obvious.

"I'll tell you what else," she said. "I think the Rats have a good chance of winning this year."

I forgot to mention, in all the years the Franklin Middle School sixth graders have been coming to River Rats games, the team has never won.

"You think so?" said Gum.

Sam pulled out her notebook. Sometimes on field trips, she used it to write down clues to a mystery we were solving. Today, though, she was checking some statistics in it.

"Potz is consistently hitting almost .400," she said. "And our starting pitcher today is Heckle. His ERA is under two for day games when the temperature is under seventy."

"Um," said Gum. We looked at each other. He was as confused as I was.

She closed her notebook and slipped it into her back pocket. "The numbers are with us," she said.

Cat and her father came up behind us. "Just promise me you won't embarrass me," said Cat quietly.

"I promise to try my best," said Mr. Duran. He gave her a kiss on the cheek.

Cat rolled her eyes. Mr. Duran headed off to talk to Mr. Gutman while Mr. Jump made his way toward the stadium.

Just then, a taxi pulled up. The back door opened, and two men climbed out.

"Hi, kids," one of them said. He was very tall and had broad shoulders and a big grin. "Here to watch the game?"

"Jimmy Heckle!" said Sam. She ran to him, grabbed his hand, and shook it. "What an honor to meet you. I was just telling my friends here how well you've been throwing."

"Big baseball fan?" asked the other man.

"Biggest in our school," said Gum. "She's a total nut for the River Rats."

Sam turned to the other man. He was much shorter and very muscular. He wasn't grinning, though. "And you're Tony Potz," she said, shaking his hand. "I can't wait to see you knock one out of the park today."

Potz frowned. "You might be waiting a long time," he said.

Sam shook her head. "Why?" she asked. "Just because you had a couple of rough days on the road?"

"A couple of rough days?" said Potz. "I'm in a slump."

"Don't say that," said Heckle.

"Right," said Sam. "A slump is a state of mind."

"Hey, Sam," I said. "Let me get a photo of the three of you."

Beaming, she got between the two players and put an arm around each of them.

"Okay," I said. "Smile!" I snapped the photo.

"Nice meeting you kids," said Heckle. "Find me after the game, and I'll give you a behind-the-scenes tour."

"This is going to be the greatest field trip ever," said Sam.

# CHAPTER TWO

# JUNK FOOD

Soon Mr. Jump came back and gave us each a ticket. Then we lined up and headed inside.

"First stop," said Mr. Duran, "the concession stand."

Gum and Sam nodded eagerly. "I love the giant pretzels," said Gum.

Mr. Duran agreed. "The cheese sauce they give you for dipping is so good," he said.

"Dad!" said Cat. "That stuff is super bad for you."

Mr. Jump overheard. "Your daughter's right, Mr. Duran," he said. "At your age, you need to watch what you eat. Why, I bet there's not a single healthy food item on that concession stand's menu."

Cat looked at the menu. "High in cholesterol," she said. "Preservatives. Artificial coloring. Artificial flavor. High in fat. High in sugar. . . ."

"High in delicious," said Gum, cutting her off.

Mr. Duran laughed.

"It's not a joke!" said Cat.

The concession stand line shuffled forward. I noticed something strange, though.

"Hey," I said. I elbowed Sam a little. "Anything seem odd about the people leaving the stand ahead of us?"

She nodded. "They don't have any food," she said. "Why were they in line if they weren't getting food?"

"They probably overheard my daughter," said Mr. Duran. "They're all worrying about preservatives and cholesterol, and they decided not to get anything."

Cat crossed her arms and frowned.

The line moved quickly. Soon we were at the counter. "I'd like a giant pretzel," said Mr. Duran. "With extra cheese sauce, please."

"Dad!" said Cat.

"Honey, a ballgame just isn't a ballgame without some junk food," said Mr. Duran.

"Sorry, sir," said the man behind the counter. "We're not serving any food at all right now."

"Huh?" he said. "You haven't been speaking to my daughter, have you?"

"Or to our gym teacher?" asked Gum.

"We're, um, having some technical problems," said the cashier.

"What does that mean?" I asked.

I snapped a photo just as a woman in a security uniform stepped up. "We got a report of a theft," she said.

"Not so loud," said the cashier. "We don't want to start a panic."

"What happened, anyway?" Sam asked.

The cashier looked around and then leaned close to all of us.

"I can't sell you any food," he said, "because the cash register has been stolen."

# CHAPTER THREE

# DELAYED INDEFINITELY

"I'm so hungry," said Gum. He pretended to be weak and leaned over till his head was practically pushing me out of my seat.

"Okay, okay!" I said. "Get off me!"

"I can't . . . " he said. "Need food . . . for energy. . . ."

"Ha, ha," said Cat. She was still pretty grumpy. "It's not like you'd get any nutrients from the concession stand food anyway."

Sam leaned back in her little stadium seat, her hand on her chin. She was thinking, probably about the stolen cash register.

I snapped a photo of her in thinking pose, with the bright-green grass of the field in the background. "Maybe we should let stadium security handle this," I said.

"Yeah," said Gum. "Let's just watch the game."

"All right, all right," said Sam. "For once, maybe I agree. I'd rather watch the Rats win on field-trip day than try to solve this crime."

Cat wasn't paying attention. She was watching Anton and his dad.

"What is it?" I asked.

"Look at those two," Cat said. "They're covered in River Rats stuff." I took a few pictures of the Gutmans in all their Rats gear.

"Yep," said Sam. "Some people feel the need to advertise what team they root for. I bet they're not as into the Rats as I am."

"No one is," said Gum.

"But they didn't have any of that stuff on the bus," said Cat.

"I guess they bought it all after we got here," I said.

"Two jerseys," said Cat, counting as she watched the Gutmans. "Two hats. Two giant foam bats. Two pennants."

"So they bought a lot of stuff," said Gum, shrugging.

"Cat's right to be suspicious," said Sam. "They must have a few hundred dollars' worth of items."

"You think they got the cash from the stolen cash register?" I asked.

Cat shrugged.

"It's worth looking into," said Sam. She pulled out her notebook and made a few notes.

"Hey, I thought we were just going to watch the game," said Gum. He flagged down a wandering vendor.

"We are," said Sam. "I'm not even leaving my seat."

Mr. Duran treated all of us to a bag of peanuts and a soda each. Cat got a bottle of water instead.

"Finally, some healthy food," she said. She cracked open a shell and popped a peanut into her mouth.

Suddenly, there was a big crackle and loud screech, like someone had plugged in a microphone someplace. One of the umpires appeared near the pitcher's mound.

"Ladies and gentlemen," he said. "I am very sorry to announce that today's game will be delayed while we investigate a theft in the stadium."

The crowd mumbled and muttered, obviously annoyed.

"Meanwhile, the police have asked no one to enter or leave the stadium," the umpire went on. "Thank you."

Then he walked off.

"Hmm," I said. "Looks like we might as well investigate."

# CHAPTER FOUR

## FIRST SUSPECT!

After a few minutes, the mascots came out and did some dances and stuff. Most fans just stayed in their seats and watched, but we had more important things to do.

Mr. Gutman got up from his seat and whispered something to Anton. Then he headed toward the concourse. He looked around as he walked, making sure Mr. Duran and Mr. Jump weren't watching.

"We'd better follow him," said Sam. We all got up.

Mr. Duran grabbed Cat's hand.

"Where are you four heading off to?" he asked.

"Um," said Cat. She was always the worst at making up excuses when we were on a case.

"I want to buy a hat," said Sam. "A Rats hat. I'm a huge fan, you know."

Mr. Duran squinted at her. "But you always wear that fedora, don't you?" he said.

"I feel like a change," Sam said.

"All right," Mr. Duran said. "Stick together out there. If you need me, my cell phone is always on."

"Okay, Dad," said Cat. "See you."

We had to hurry. Mr. Gutman had a big head start. We rushed to the concourse and spotted him getting onto an escalator.

"Where is he going?" I asked.

"We're going to find out," said Sam. We watched until Mr. Gutman was nearly at the top. Then we hopped onto the escalator too.

"He went to the left," I said, pointing.

Upstairs, there were no big open doorways leading to the seats, like on the level below. There were no concession stands, either. There were lots of doors, though. We followed Mr. Gutman around the circular stadium, staying far behind so he wouldn't see us.

"These must be offices," Sam said. "Officials only, probably."

Up ahead, Mr. Gutman stopped at a door. We hid around the corner and watched. He looked around, then opened the door just enough to slip inside. I snapped a photo just as he closed the door behind him.

"Come on," Sam said, and she ran to the door. We followed.

"Look at this," Sam said, pointing at the door. A sign on the door read "Authorized Personnel Only."

"Hmm," said Gum. "I wonder if Mr. Gutman is authorized."

I took a photo of the door. "Beats me," I said. "He sure was acting suspicious."

Sam put a hand on the door handle.

"Sam!" said Cat. "What are you doing? We can't go in there!"

"I just want to take a peek," said Sam. She tried opening the door. It was locked.

Suddenly a firm hand dropped on my shoulder. It was a huge man in a security uniform.

"What do you think
you're doing?"
he asked.

# STRIKING OUT

"We weren't going in!" I protested. He let go of our necks.

"Oh, no?" he said. He had this big, mean grin on his face. "Then why was she trying to open the door?"

He shoved between us and grabbed the door handle. "Locked," he said. "What are you doing up here anyway? Aren't you with the field trip?"

"Yes, sir," said Cat. "But our, um, friend's father came upstairs, and we were curious, so . . ."

"So you followed him?" said the security guard. He crossed his arms. "That's not very polite."

"He's our chaperone!" said Gum. "And he went in here," Gum added.

The guard tried the handle again. "How did he do that?" asked the guard. "Like I said, it's locked."

"He probably locked it after he went in," I said. I lifted my camera and turned on the display to show him. "Look, I took a photo of —"

But he just waved me off and said, "I'm not interested in seeing your photographs, kid. Taking secret photos is every bit as impolite as following someone."

He took me by the shoulders and turned me. Then he pointed for us to leave.

"Find the escalator back down to your seats," the guard said. "And don't let me catch you up here again."

What choice did we have? Heads hanging, we went back to our seats. Mr. Duran smiled at us and waved.

"Are you eating something?" Cat said.

He smiled even bigger, but he didn't say anything.

"Dad!" Cat said. "What are you eating?"

Sam snuck around behind him and grabbed a candy-bar wrapper he'd been hiding in his hand.

"Aha!" she said, holding it up. "A Gooey Choco Pop Bar."

"Ooh, I love those," said Gum.

Mr. Jump watched Mr. Duran chewing.

"You should be thankful the concession stand is closed," Mr. Jump said. "Trust me, your health is sure thankful!" He got up and stomped off.

Cat covered her face in embarrassment.

"Boy, that was rude," said Mr. Duran when he was done chewing his candy bar. Sam and Gum and I nodded in agreement. Cat didn't agree.

"He's right!" Cat shouted, stomping her foot. "You eat like a pig! I'm glad the concession stand is closed. That's lots of animal fat, cholesterol, preservatives, and other poisons that you'll never get your hands on!"

"We should go talk to her," I said. After all, Cat was our best friend.

"We sure should," Sam said. She pulled out her notebook and wrote something.

I looked over her shoulder, and I couldn't believe what I saw.

"'Catalina Duran'," I read out loud. "'Prime suspect'!"

Sam put the notebook in her pocket. "That's right," she said.

"How can you say that?" I asked. "Cat would never steal!"

Sam crossed her arms. "She's on the list," she said.

"I guess we should ask her questions," said Gum.

"You too?" I asked, shaking my head. "It would be completely unlike her."

Gum shrugged. "Sam knows a lot about crime investigation," he said. "If she thinks we should have Cat on the list, I guess we should."

* * *

We found Cat sitting on a bench next to a souvenir stand. She looked like she'd been crying.

"Hi," she said. "Sorry for being a baby."

"Don't worry about it," I said. I sat down next to her.

"Cat," said Sam. "We have to ask you some questions."

"Huh?" said Cat.

"Where were you at exactly 11:42 this morning?" Sam said.

"What are you talking about?" asked Cat. "I was standing with you in front of the stadium."

"Mm-hm," said Sam. "Can you prove that? I was talking to Heckle and Potz. If you'd slipped away, none of us would have noticed."

"Wait a minute," said Cat, standing up. "Are you asking me these questions because I'm a suspect? Do you think I stole the cash register?"

"I don't," I said.

Cat looked at Sam and Gum. "Well?" she said. "What do you two think?"

Neither answered.

"Why would I steal some dumb cash register?" Cat said. She was about to cry again, so I put my arm around her shoulders.

Sam pulled out her notebook and flipped through it. "'Motive,'" she read. "'She doesn't like it when her dad eats unhealthy food. No concession stand means no unhealthy food.'"

Cat stared at Sam as Sam put away the notebook.

"I —" said Cat, but she couldn't finish. Instead she ran off.

"Nice going, Sam," I said.

"I'm sorry," she said, but I could tell she wasn't. "We have to look into every lead."

I chased after Cat. I caught up with her around the bend in the concourse just before she ducked into the women's room. Good thing too, since I wouldn't have been able to follow her any farther.

"Wait, Cat!" I shouted.

She stopped. "What do you want?" she yelled.

"Hey, don't be mad at me," I said. "I know you'd never do anything like that."

Cat sniffed. I guess she'd been crying again. I couldn't blame her. "Thanks," she said.

"I think we should get back to investigating Mr. Gutman," I said. "He's a more likely suspect."

"Maybe," said Cat. Then her face lit up. "Hey, I just thought of something."

"What?" I asked.

"Who do we know who really needs money?" she asked.

"Lots of people," I said. "I'd like a new camera, for example. Gum has been wanting to buy the new GameBox."

"No," said Cat. "I said 'needs money,' not 'wants money.'"

It took me a second, but I got it: Cat meant Peter Laurie, the boy in our class whose father hadn't been able to find a job.

"And there he goes," said Cat, looking over my shoulder. I turned around. Peter was heading up the escalator.

# CHAPTER SEVEN

# THE CHASE

We caught up to Peter just where I thought we would: outside the door Mr. Gutman had gone in.

I snapped a photo of Peter trying the door handle. As I did, Cat called out to him, "Hey, Peter. Whatcha doing?"

Peter spun around to see who was calling him. When he saw us, he took off running down the hallway, right down the stairs to the concourse.

"After him!" Cat shouted.

Peter was fast! Luckily, he was also almost as tall as Sam, and that meant his red baseball cap wasn't too hard to spot in the crowd as he ran.

"There he goes!" I said, pointing at the red cap. Cat and I weaved through the crowd.

Then we lost him. Cat and I jumped up and down, trying to find any sign of Peter. But it was hopeless.

"Now what?" she asked. I shrugged. Then we heard Sam's voice.

"Hey, where are you going in such a hurry, Peter?" she shouted.

"Just get out of my way," Peter snapped.

The voices weren't far off. I pulled Cat through the crowd. We found Sam and Gum blocking Peter's path.

"You caught him!" said Cat as we jogged over. "Nice going."

Sam's face lit up. "Cat," she said. "Gum and I have been looking all over for you."

"You have?" Cat asked.

Sam nodded. "I just wanted to apologize," she said. "I feel like a jerk. I'm sorry. And so is Gum."

"Yeah," said Gum. "I'm sorry too. I mean, it was Sam's idea, but I'm sorry I didn't tell her to stuff it."

Sam sneered at him. He smiled back and inched away.

"Anyway," said Sam, "I hope you can forgive me. It was silly of me to think that."

With us distracted by Sam and Cat making up, Peter started to tiptoe away. Gum grabbed the back of his shirt.

"Not so fast, Peter," said Gum.

"So," I said, stepping up to Peter. "What were you doing up there?"

"None of your business!" said Peter.

"Why were you being so sneaky?" asked Cat.

"None of your business, either!" said Peter.

"What do you know about what's behind that door?" asked Sam. "Is that where you and Mr. Gutman stashed the stolen cash?"

"Stolen cash?" said Peter. "Wait a minute. Do you think I stole the missing cash register?"

"We all know that your family needs money," said Gum. "If you confess and return the money and the register, I'm sure you'd get off easy."

"I didn't take it!" said Peter. "My dad lost his job, but that it doesn't mean I'd do something like that.

"Then what were you doing up there?" asked Sam.

"I was hungry," Peter said.

"We're all hungry," said Gum.

"Then you should go up there and sneak in too," said Peter. "Behind that door is all the food you can eat."

# CHAPTER EIGHT

## BUSTED!

"There's food in there?" I asked. "We thought it was an office."

Peter shook his head. "You can actually see a little of it from the seats," he said. "I saw Anton and his dad in there."

"With food?" Gum asked.

"Yup," said Peter. "Come on. I'll show you."

We headed back upstairs with Peter. At the top, we ducked down around a bend and watched the door. Before long, it opened.

"Here they come," whispered Peter.

Mr. Gutman's head popped out. He looked around for a second to make sure the coast was clear. Then he stepped out — carrying a foot-long sub sandwich.

"Where did he get that?" asked Gum.

"Those are my dad's favorite," said Cat.

"Shh," said Peter. Mr. Gutman was walking toward us. We shuffled out of sight and watched him go down the escalator.

"You were right," said Sam. She shook his hand. "You're pretty good at this sleuth stuff. Maybe we should hang out more often."

Peter blushed.

"I'm sorry, Peter," said Cat. "We shouldn't have accused you. And I should have known better, since my friends had just accused me."

"It's okay," said Peter.

"Everyone down," snapped Gum. "The door's opening again."

Anton came out. The five of us surrounded him in a flash.

He was so startled that he dropped everything he'd been carrying: two hot dogs, a giant cup of soda, a bag of chips, and an ice cream sundae in a mini plastic baseball helmet.

It all splattered onto the carpet and made a huge mess. Some of the soda splashed onto Gum's pants — and Anton's.

"Ugh, look what you dorks made me do!" he shouted.

"Where did you get all that food?" Sam said, glaring at him.

"Back off, beanpole," Anton said.

"Just answer us," Gum said. He blocked Anton's path. "Where did you get that food? The concession stand is still closed."

"Pff," Anton said. "I wouldn't eat that concession stand food anyway. That food is for losers and dorks. Like you five!" He laughed his head off. "Nope, I got it in there."

He thumbed toward the door.

"What's in there?" Cat asked. "Is it a private restaurant?"

"Something like that," said Anton. "It's my dad's company's private box. It has the best view of the field, *and* it has all-you-can-eat food."

"Then why all the sneaking around?" I asked.

"The way your dad has been creeping all over, you'd think that place was top secret," added Gum.

"If everyone knew about the food," Anton said, "then everyone would want some."

"So why don't you let the rest of the class inside?" Cat asked. "We're all starving, and there's nowhere else to get food."

"Why should we?" Anton said. "The rest of the class doesn't work for my dad's company."

"Neither do you," Sam said.

"No, but my name is Gutman," Anton said. "And that means one day, it'll be *my* company. Now step aside."

What could we do? He wasn't guilty of stealing the cash register. He was just guilty of being a selfish dweeb. We let him go.

Sam pulled out her notebook. "That's that," she said. "No more suspects. I'm stumped."

# CHAPTER NINE

# LISTENING IN

I spotted Mr. Jump coming up the escalator. "Quick," I said to the others, "hide."

We watched our teacher march right into an office near the top of the escalator. We shuffled along the wall until we were right outside the door, so we could listen. A sign on this door said "Pauline Polka, Stadium Manager."

"Do you guys do this a lot?" asked Peter. "I mean, sneak around and listen in on teachers' conversations?"

"Kind of," Gum said. "We're . . . part-time detectives."

"Cool," said Peter.

Suddenly, Mr. Jump began to shout. "I'm afraid I must insist!" he yelled.

"I'm sorry, Mr. Jump," said a woman. I figured it was Ms. Polka. "We have a strict no-refunds policy once you've entered the stadium."

"But the game hasn't even started!" Mr. Jump said. "I have to have these kids back at school by three. At this rate, they won't see even half the game."

"I'm very sorry," said Ms. Polka. "There's simply nothing I can do."

"Well, let me warn you, then," said Mr. Jump. "I intend to write a very strongly worded letter."

"If you must," said Ms. Polka.

"My letter will also address the poor quality of the food in this stadium," Mr. Jump continued.

"I'm sorry you feel that way," said Ms. Polka.

"Humph!" said Mr. Jump. Then we heard his heavy footsteps heading toward the door. We dove out of sight.

"Boy, he's angry," said Peter.

We all nodded, except Cat. "Well," she said quietly. "He's right, you know. They should offer healthier food here."

"You're probably right, Cat," said Sam. "But more importantly, you know what this means, right?"

We all grinned.

"We have a new number-one suspect," I said. "Let's follow Mr. Jump."

# CHAPTER TEN

# OUT OF THE PARK

We followed Mr. Jump down to the concourse, all the way around to the back, and out to the parking lot.

Mr. Jump jogged between cars. He stayed low, like he didn't want anyone to see him.

When he reached the bus, he pried the door open and climbed on. Quietly, we followed him aboard. He was way in the back, down on his hands and knees, reaching under the very back seat.

We tiptoed up the aisle. Mr. Jump muttered to himself, "Where is that dumb thing?"

When we were right behind him, Sam cleared her throat. Mr. Jump knocked his head on the bottom of the seat. He got to his feet, rubbing his head.

"What are you doing here?" he said. "You kids should be inside. Where are the chaperones, anyway?"

"What are *you* doing here, Mr. Jump?" I asked.

"Yeah," said Cat. "Did you lose something under the seat?"

"Of course not," Mr. Jump said. "I just, um . . . I'm just trying to find, well . . ."

"I'll just take a look," said Gum. He dropped to the floor and crawled all the way under the seat.

"Aha!" he said. He scooted out, holding a small, black case.

"Is this what you were looking for?" he asked.

"That?" said Mr. Jump. "Of course not. I've never seen that before in my life."

"Well," I said, "it's definitely not a cash register."

"I'll just open it up," Gum said.

"No!" Mr. Jump said. He grabbed for the case. "Don't open that!"

Gum pulled it away quickly. "Why not?" he asked, smiling. "Am I about to find the missing concession stand money?"

"The money?" Mr. Jump repeated. "Why would the missing money be in there?"

"It was you, wasn't it?" Sam asked. "You had the motive and the opportunity."

"That's ridiculous," said Mr. Jump. "Why would I want to steal from the concession stand?"

"To shut it down!" said Cat. "You're as concerned with healthy eating as I am."

"That's true," said Mr. Jump slowly. But his face turned bright red.

Gum unlatched the case.

"Give that to me!" Mr. Jump said. He grabbed for the case and it fell open. The contents spilled all over. There were cheesy crackers, potato chips, candy bars, and a can of soda.

"Mr. Jump," Cat said. "Is this your junk food?"

He stared at his sneakers. "Yes," he admitted. "I hid it there so no one would know I'm a . . . a . . ."

Tears exploded from his eyes. "I'm a junk food junkie!" he said.

He dropped his head and cried. Cat put an arm around his shoulders. "There, there," she said. "My dad is a junk food junkie too. I know how hard it is to quit."

Mr. Jump nodded. "It really is," he said.

"So now what do we do?" Sam whispered while Cat comforted our gym teacher.

"Let's take a look at Egg's photos," Gum said.

I clicked on the display and started at the beginning. The first few photos were of the stadium. I clicked right past the one of Heckle and Potz with Sam.

"Wait a second," Sam said. "Go back."

"Here?" I said.

She nodded and leaned in close. It was the photo of her with the two players.

"Potz sure looks grumpy," Sam said.

"He's in a slump," Gum said. "I'd be grumpy too."

"I just realized something," Sam said. "The concession stand is closed, so we're all focused on food. But what else happened when the register went missing?"

"The game was delayed," Cat said.

"Bingo," Sam said. "Come on. Follow me."

* * *

Sam led us right to the seats over the home dugout. "Hey, Heckle!" she shouted.

The pitcher stood up. "Hi," he said. "Sam, right?"

"Yup," Sam said, grinning. "So, I was thinking, since we're not doing anything else, how about that tour now?"

# CHAPTER ELEVEN

# A HOME RUN

Heckle led us down a long hallway. It was pretty dark, only lit by these old lights on the low ceiling. At the end of the hall, Heckle opened a door.

"After you," he said.

We went past him and into a gleaming, bright, white room. It was big, with a dry-erase whiteboard all along one wall. Along the opposite wall were dozens of lockers.

"The home-team locker room," Heckle said as he followed us in.

"I can't believe how clean it is," said Gum. "I figured it would be kind of gross."

"Yeah," said Cat. "I thought it would be full of dirty uniforms and stinky, old towels and stuff."

Heckle laughed. "Some clubs have locker rooms like that," he said. "But we have a little more pride in what we do."

Sam wasn't paying attention at all. She was looking under benches and behind shower curtains.

"Looking for something?" Heckle asked.

She pointed at a closed door next to Heckle. "What's in there?" she asked.

"That's just the laundry room," he said. "It'll be full of those stinky, old towels your friend mentioned."

"Can we see them?" asked Sam.

"What?" Gum asked. "Why do you want to see some nasty, old towels?"

Sam shushed him. She smiled at Heckle and batted her eyes. Honestly, it was the girliest thing I'd ever seen her do. But it worked.

"Well," said Heckle, "if you want to see the laundry room that badly . . ."

He pulled open the door. It was dark inside, so he reached in and hit the light switch. Then he stepped to the side. "There you go," he said. "Like I said, it's not too interesting."

Sam ran in. There were washing machines and dryers, and a big, canvas tub on wheels, full of dirty towels. The clean towels were on metal shelves lining all four walls.

"I was sure it would be in here," said Sam.

Something caught my eye.

"That towel on top of the laundry tub," I said. "It looks pretty clean to me."

Sam grabbed a corner of the towel between two fingers. She leaned forward, her face scrunched up, and sniffed the towel. Then she smiled. "Bleach," she said in a whisper.

"Stop!" someone shouted behind us. We all turned to look. It was Potz, the slumping slugger. He ran toward us and practically shoved Sam away from the laundry tub.

"What are you doing in here?" he snapped at Sam. "This is off-limits to fans."

Heckle stepped into the laundry room. "Take it easy, Potz," he said. He smiled at Sam and the rest of us. "He's just anxious for the game to finally start."

"Oh, I'm not so sure he is," I said. I slipped in behind Heckle, where Potz couldn't reach me. Then I grabbed the corner of the clean towel and pulled it off. Under it was the missing cash register.

Heckle gasped.

"I knew it!" Sam shouted.

"How'd that get there?" Potz asked nervously. He smiled and pretended to laugh. "That is so weird."

Heckle stared at him. "Potz, you did this?" he said. "You stole the register?"

Potz turned away.

"Why, Potz?" Heckle asked.

Potz didn't answer.

Sam explained, "He figured if the game didn't start, he wouldn't have to hit."

Potz nodded sadly. "Maybe if I got a day off, it would be enough to break the slump," he said.

Cat pulled out her phone and made a call. "Dad?" she said. "It's me. Grab a security guard and come to the home-team locker room. I'll explain when you get here."

"Aw," Potz said. "Do you have to turn me in? The money's all there. I wasn't going to keep it."

Two security guards burst in. Behind them was a man in a trench coat.

"Detective Jones!" said Gum. Detective Jones often showed up when we were working a case. We've solved a lot of crimes together.

"How did I know I'd find you here?" said the detective. "Who's going to tell me what's going on here?"

Sam and I explained everything to the detective. He handcuffed Potz and led him away.

* * *

The umpire with the microphone was on the pitcher's mound when we returned to our seats. "We're about ready to start," he said. "First, we have one correction to your program. Starting at first base will not be Tony Potz as scheduled. Subbing for him will be Dwight Smith."

"I guess the slump is over after all," I said.

"Yeah," said Gum. "Maybe he'll hit a little better for the River City Prison Team."

## literary news

# MYSTERIOUS WRITER REVEALED!

Steve Brezenoff lives in Minneapolis, Minnesota, with his wife, Beth, and their son, Sam. Besides writing books, he enjoys playing video games, riding his bicycle, and helping middle-school students work on their writing skills. Steve's ideas almost always come to him in his dreams, so he does his best writing in his pajamas.

## arts & entertainment

# ARTIST IS KEY TO SOLVING MYSTERY, SAY POLICE

Marcos Calo lives happily in A Coruña, Spain, with his wife, Patricia (who is also an illustrator), and their daughter, Claudia. When Marcos and Patricia aren't drawing, they like to go on long walks by the sea. They also watch a lot of films and eat Nutella sandwiches. Yum!

# A Detective's Dictionary

**accused** (uh-KYOOZD)–said that someone did something wrong

**authorized** (AW-thuh-rized)–having permission to do something

**chaperone** (SHAP-uh-rohn)–an adult who protects the safety of young people at an event such as a field trip

**concourse** (KON-kohrs)–an area where many people pass

**intimidating** (in-TIM-uh-date-ing)–frightening

**investigate** (in-VESS-tuh-gate)–to find out as much as possible about something, such as a crime

**motive** (MOH-tiv)–a reason for doing something

**sleuth** (SLOOTH)–a detective

**slump** (SLUHMP)–a sudden drop or decline

**souvenir** (soo-vuh-NIHR)–an object that you keep to remind you of a place, a person, or an event

**suspect** (SUHS-pekt)–person who may be responsible for a crime

**technical** (TEK-nuh-kuhl)–related to machines or science

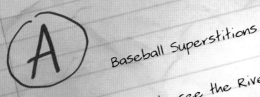

Edward Garrison

6th-Grade Gym

A

Baseball Superstitions

On our field trip to see the River City Rats, Tony Potz stole the cash register to delay the game. He thought if the game was cancelled, his slump might be broken. To people who aren't fans of baseball, this plan might sound crazy. But lovers of the sport know that baseball players tend to be very superstitious.

Many players purposely step on the foul line when they take the field for good luck. Others purposely avoid it. Some players always follow a certain routine on game days. Wade Boggs, one of the most superstitious players ever, always ate fried chicken before every game.

Some players have good luck charms. New York Mets player Turk Wendell wore a necklace that was made out of animal teeth for luck whenever he pitched.

One of the most famous and longest superstitions in baseball was the Curse of the Bambino. Winner of five World Series titles, the Boston Red Sox were one of the best teams in the league until they sold the Bambino, Babe Ruth, to the New York Yankees in 1920.

The Yankees went on to be one of the most successful teams in baseball. Meanwhile, the Red Sox didn't win another World Series until 2004 – nearly eighty years later!

Edward – Great job! Did you happen to come across any superstitions involving junk food? Any at all?

—Mr. Jump

# FURTHER INVESTIGATIONS

CASE #FTM17EGRCR

1. In this book, the sixth-grade gym class (including me) went on a field trip. What field trips have you gone on? Which one was your favorite, and why?

2. What's the best part of going to a baseball game?

3. Who else could have been a suspect in this mystery? Talk about your reasons.

## IN YOUR OWN DETECTIVE'S NOTEBOOK . . .

1. Cat wants her dad to stop eating junk food. Pretend you are Cat and write a letter to your dad, trying to convince him to give up junk food.

2. Who is your favorite character in the book? Why? Write about that person.

3. This book is a mystery story. Write your own mystery story!